12-94

To the Kesting Family!

Love, Aunt Chris

The
PiGGY
iN THe PUDDLE

The Piggy in The Puddle

Words by CHARLOTTE POMERANTZ
Pictures by JAMES MARSHALL

ALADDIN BOOKS
Macmillan Publishing Company • New York

Aladdin Books
Macmillan Publishing Company
866 Third Avenue, New York, NY 10022
Collier Macmillan Canada, Inc.

First Aladdin Books edition 1989

Printed in the United States of America

A hardcover edition of *The Piggy in the Puddle* is available from
Macmillan Publishing Company.

10 9 8 7 6 5 4

Library of Congress Cataloging-in-Publication Data

Pomerantz, Charlotte.
The piggy in the puddle/words by Charlotte Pomerantz; pictures
by James Marshall.—1st Aladdin books ed.
p.   cm.
Summary: Unable to persuade a young pig from frolicking in the
mud, her family finally joins her for a mud party.
ISBN 0-689-71293-6
[1. Pigs—Fiction. 2. Mud—Fiction. 3. Stories in rhyme.]
I. Marshall, James, 1942- ill. II. Title.
PZ8.3.P564Pi 1989
[E]—dc19   88-8368   CIP   AC

For Gabrielle, Daniel and Jennifer — C. P.

For Eloise Clifton — J. M.

See the piggy,
See the puddle,
See the muddy little puddle.
See the piggy in the middle
Of the muddy little puddle.
See her dawdle, see her diddle
In the muddy, muddy middle.
See her waddle, plump and little,
In the very merry middle.

See her daddy,
Fuddy-duddy, fuddy-duddy, fuddy-duddy.
"Don't you get all muddy,
Muddy, muddy, muddy, muddy.
You are much too plump and little
To be in the muddy middle.
Mud is squishy, mud is squashy,
Mud is oh so squishy-squashy.
What you need is lots of soap."
But the piggy answered,
"Squishy-squashy, squishy-squashy—NOPE!"

See her mommy,
Fiddle-faddle, fiddle-faddle, fiddle-faddle.
"Get out of there—skedaddle,
Daddle, daddle, daddle, daddle.
You are much too plump and little
To be in the muddy middle.
Mud is mooshy, mud is squooshy,
Mud is oh so mooshy-squooshy.
What you need is lots of soap."
But the piggy answered,
"Mooshy-squooshy, mooshy-squooshy—NOPE!"

See her brother,
Silly billy, silly billy, silly billy.
"Do not waddle willy-nilly,
Willy-nilly, willy-nilly.
You are much too plump and little
To be in the muddy middle.
Mud is oofy, mud is poofy,
Mud is oh so oofy-poofy.
What you need is lots of soap."

But the piggy answered,
"Oofy-poofy, oofy-poofy — NOPE!"

Now they all stood in a huddle,
Right beside the muddy puddle.
And they looked into the puddle—
What a muddy, muddy muddle!

There was piggy, plump and little,
In the very merry middle.
She was waddling, she was paddling,
She was diving way down derry.
She was wiggling, she was giggling,
She was very, very merry.
Said the mother,
"Little piggy, you have made me very mad."
Said the father,
"Little piggy, you have made me very sad."
"Little piggy," said the brother,
"You are very, very bad."
Said the piggy,
"Squishy-squashy, mooshy-squooshy, very bad."

"Dear, oh dear," said piggy's mother.
"What's a mother pig to do?"
She thought and thought and thought and thought—
And then, of course, she knew.
She said, "I bet my feet get wet."
And — jumped — in — too!

See two piggies in the puddle,
In the muddy little puddle.
See the piggy and her mommy
In the muddy little puddle.
"Me oh my," said piggy's father.
"What's a father pig to do?"
He thought and thought and thought and thought —
And then, of course, he knew.
He said, "I bet my tail gets wet."
And — jumped — in — too!

See three piggies in the puddle,
In the muddy little puddle.
See mommy, daddy, piggy
In the muddy little puddle.
"Boo-hoo-hoo," cried piggy's brother.
"Whatever shall I do?"
He thought, but not for very long,
Because, of course, he knew.
He held his nose and yelled, "Here goes!"
And — jumped — in — too!

See four piggies in the puddle,
In the muddy little puddle.
See the piggies in the middle
Of the muddy little puddle.
See them diddle, big and little,
In the very merry middle.
Said the daddy, "Mud is squishy,
Mud is oh so squishy-squashy."
Said the mommy, "Mud is mooshy,
Mud is oh so mooshy-squooshy."
Said the brother, "Mud is oofy,
Mud is oh so oofy-poofy."

Said the piggy,
"Squishy-squashy, mooshy-squooshy, oofy-poofy.
Indeed," said little piggy,
"I think we need some soap."
But the other piggies answered,
"Oofy-poofy — NOPE!"

So they all dove way down derry,
And were very, very merry.